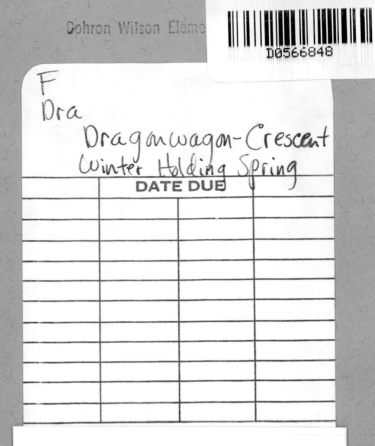

F
Dra

Dragonwagon-Crescent
Winter Holding Spring

DATE DUE

WINTER
HOLDING
SPRING

by Crescent Dragonwagon

illustrated by Ronald Himler

Macmillan Publishing Company   New York

For Mattie Mae Cox,
who knows that spring always comes

Macmillan Publishing Company
866 Third Avenue, New York, NY 10022
Collier Macmillan Canada, Inc.
First Edition
Printed in the United States of America

10 9 8 7 6 5 4 3 2 1

The text of this book is set in 13 point Goudy Old Style.
The illustrations are rendered in pencil on paper.

Library of Congress Cataloging-in-Publication Data
Dragonwagon, Crescent.
Winter holding spring/by Crescent Dragonwagon;
illustrated by Ronald Himler. — 1st ed.   p.   cm.
Summary: In discussing her mother's death with her father,
eleven-year-old Sarah comes to see that in endings
there are new beginnings, that in winter there is the
promise of spring, and that everything comes full circle.
ISBN 0-02-733122-9
[1. Death — Fiction. 2. Parent and child — Fiction.
3. Seasons — Fiction.] I. Himler, Ronald, ill. II. Title.
PZ7.D7824Wj   1990   [Fic] — dc19   88-13747   CIP   AC

In the middle of summer, Sarah and her father discover fall.

They are in the garden, filling a basket with tomatoes and peppers. It's August, and so hot the air itself coats their skin. Everything sticks. Sarah's father's bare back gleams with sweat. Her own face, a little sunburned, shines in the heat. Every round tomato, heavy with juice, is warm with sun, warm as a baby's cheek, warm as a living thing.

It is hot, *soooooo* hot.

Sarah squints up at the blue sky bleached white by August. She sees, floating lazily from side to side, a leaf from the black walnut tree, taking its time to come down and rest, bright yellow, on the green leaves of the bell pepper plant.

She picks it up.

"Look," says Sarah to her father, showing him the yellow leaf. "Look."

"Ah," says her father, looking. "In the middle of summer, there's always fall."

Later, they are in the kitchen. Her father, standing, stirs the steaming, cooking tomatoes in the red enamel pot. Sarah sits at the kitchen table, too hot to move. She holds her bangs up off her face and lets them drop.

"Can we go out to the lake *soon?*" she asks.

"Soon," her father promises. "Soon as I finish canning these tomatoes."

Quart jars, lined up like soldiers, wait on the counter. A steaming kettle, midnight blue and dotted with tiny white stars like a summer night sky, hot and full of boiling water, waits on the stove by the red pot.

Sarah frowns. She lifts the hair up from the back of her neck, then lets it fall. She remembers her mother, canning tomatoes with her hair pinned up to the top of her head, anchored with two crossed chopsticks. She asks her father, "Does it mean things are always ending?"

Her father turns from the stove and looks at her.

"You mean like the leaf?" he asks her. "Like fall right in the middle of summer?"

Sarah nods.

"Well, yes," he says, "it does. But it also means things are always beginning."

"Oh," says Sarah. Then she says, "Do some tomatoes with basil, Daddy."

"Only if you run out and get me some."

Sarah takes the orange-handled scissors, goes back to the garden, snip-snip-snips the sweet-spicy, bright green basil with its tender, creased, green leaves. She sees another yellow leaf, floating, falling, and she catches it in her hand.

Then she brings the basil, a bright green bunch of it, in to her father. Basil was her mother's favorite herb.

When twelve quart jars of tomatoes have been canned, six with basil leaves, Sarah and her father go out to the lake.

One Saturday morning, the sky has turned from bleached white to a blue as bright as the blue of a postcard sky. The air is not heavy but light, puffed with breeze, delicate, fresh. When Sarah wakes up, the curtains on the window by the bed, which have been still all summer long, are blowing out over her, like skirts of ladies dancing.

Sarah lies in bed with her eyes open, thinking of a twirly skirt her mother used to wear, a skirt the blue of a swimming pool. Then she just thinks about her mother.

For breakfast, Sarah's father makes pancakes. He puts chopped apples in them.

"Isn't the air delicious?" he asks her, smiling. "Mmmm." He breathes in.

"Yes," says Sarah. Saturday, she thinks, is the best day of the week, her and her father's day together, without school or homework or his going to work or anything.

"Today," announces her father, "we're going to North River Mall to get you some new school clothes."

Sarah likes to shop. At the mall, she picks out clothes she thinks she would like and goes into the dressing room by herself to try them on, while her father sits outside in a blue chair, reading the paper. When she comes out and models for her father, he always puts the paper down. He discusses each piece of clothing with her very seriously.

"Turn around," he says. "Let me see the back." Or, "I like that color." Or, "Is that comfortable?" Or, "It's cute, but will you really wear it?"

Sarah and her father pick out a pumpkin-colored corduroy skirt and jacket, a dark brown turtleneck, a knit sweater flecked with little bits of orange and brown and green and yellow and gold, and a pleated plaid skirt of the same colors. They also buy yellow socks, yellow tights, brown tights, and a pair of saddle shoes with white toes and brown middles.

"You have good taste," her father compliments her. "I like your colors. They are just right for fall. Now, will you come and help me pick out a tie in the men's department?"

Sarah and her father pick out a brown tie with a pattern of tiny embroidered gold and green geese flying.

They walk out to the parking lot. The bags they carry rustle as they walk. They put the bags in the trunk and get in the car. By now, it is a little hot, but there is still a sweet-smelling breeze.

Driving, Sarah's father asks her, "Remember that vest your mother used to wear a lot? The knit one from Vermont with the cows?"

"Yes," says Sarah. "It had geese, too."

"Yes," says her father. "Geese and cows..."

"And a farmhouse and trees and a blue sky and a yellow sun and little stars..." says Sarah.

"And a moon, a tiny fingernail of a moon, on the back," says her father.

They come out of the parking lot and turn right onto the main road.

"She might have worn it on a day like today," says Sarah. "At least, this morning, before it got hot."

Her father nods. "Yeah, she would have," he agrees. "With jeans, or maybe a blue-jean skirt."

"A twirly kind of a skirt," says Sarah.

"Yes," says her father. "She liked those twirly skirts."

They wait at the red light.

Without looking at Sarah, her father says softly, "I miss her."

"I miss her too," says Sarah. She doesn't look at her father as she says this, but straight ahead, at the red light, high above on a wire, swinging slightly in the breeze. It changes to green.

Sarah and her father drive past the McDonald's, the Toys-R-Us, the unfinished furniture place, the stereo store. Then they turn off onto Crossover Road, where they pass houses instead of stores, where there are trees and gardens and backyards.

"Will you look at that, so soon," says Sarah's father, pointing to an oak whose leaves, on one side, are already bright red.

"Remember that leaf we found in the summer, Daddy, that yellow leaf?" Sarah asks. "The day we were in the garden, and later you canned some tomatoes and then we went to the lake?"

"Oh, yes," says her father. "It was so hot. Hard to believe that was only six weeks ago."

"Do you remember what you said, about fall being in the middle of summer?" Sarah asks.

Her father turns from the wheel and the road for a moment to look at Sarah, nodding.

"Well, now it's fall...." Sarah pauses.

"Yes?" says her father.

"Well, is winter in the middle of fall somewhere?"

"Surely," says her father.

"Where?" asks Sarah.

"Oh, I don't know," says her father. "But if you look, you'll see it somewhere or someway or other, if not today, then one day soon."

Sarah and her father pass the houses on Crossover Road, and they come to the two or three small farms still left out that way.

"Look!" says Sarah suddenly.

Out the car window, to their left, is a field of pumpkins, bright orange and big as beach balls, stretched out among the scraggly green vines.

"Well, there you are," says her father. "Winter in fall."

"Not really, Daddy," Sarah says. "Pumpkins are still fall. They're Halloween."

"Yes, but they're also Thanksgiving, pumpkin pies."

Sarah thinks about it. "And Thanksgiving is almost Hanukkah and Christmas, and that's winter." She is still, thinking about it. Finally she says, "It's so sad. Nothing gets to just *be*. It's always turning into the next thing."

"Yes," says her father. "But it also is happy, because nothing just *ends* without beginning the next thing at the same time, do you see?"

Sarah nodded, but she did not fully agree. If everything is always ending but beginning at the same time, she thinks, looking out the window at the fall-blue sky, the countryside brushed with gold, then what was the beginning when Mommy died? That was an ending...just an ending. And what could ever, ever, be happy about that?

Sarah presses her face hard to the window.

At home that night, Sarah takes her new clothes out of their crisp paper bags, unfolds them, taking out the tissue paper. She lays them in a row on her bed, admires them, and begins hanging them up, one by one.

But the plaid skirt is so pretty, with its big squares of gold and pumpkin and deep brown and leaf green, that Sarah takes off her pajama bottoms and tries it on again. Then, alone in her bedroom, in front of the mirror, in her pajama top and the new plaid skirt, she twirls. The plaid material flies out around her, like wings, like a lady's skirt at a dance.

One Saturday in February, Sarah and her father go to the library. While he is at the reference section doing something for his work, Sarah collects books she thinks would be interesting and carries them to a round library table. She spreads them out around her to help her decide which she will take out. She always picks far too many to take at one time, so she has to narrow it down.

There are several ways to decide about books: looking at the picture on the book cover under its shiny transparent wrapper, then reading the description of the book and the author. She likes it if there is a picture of the author. She stares at the picture and thinks about what the author might be like, and she reads the sentences describing the author. But what really decides Sarah is this: She opens the book, giving each one two tries. She first reads the first paragraph of the book, and then she opens the book to somewhere in the middle, and reads a few paragraphs on whatever page she opened to. If these paragraphs interest her, she takes the book home.

Sarah's favorite books have old houses in them, with rooms no one has discovered and hidden passages. The main characters are always smart girls, who are usually sent away to live in the old houses, where they have to overcome something — relatives who don't like them, or ghosts, or evil spirits, or eccentric neighbors who have a secret to hide that the heroines discover by accident. Sometimes they solve mysteries.

Occasionally, the girls are dancers, or keep diaries and want to be writers, or paint watercolors. Sometimes they are psychic. Sometimes they are skeptical about the supernatural, but by the end of the book they know that they really did see a spirit or travel back through time.

But this day, one of the books Sarah has picked begins: *She was eleven the year her mother died. And it was impossible, of course, that anything could ever be the same.*

Without looking at the author's picture or opening the book at random to read any more, Sarah gets up from the table and takes the book back to the shelf where she thinks she found it. According to the rules of the library, you are not supposed to reshelve books yourself, but to let the librarians do it. But Sarah simply cannot leave that book lying around. She never wants to see it again.

Instead, she finds a book about a girl named Tamara who spends the summer in an old Victorian mansion on the coast of Maine with an aunt she has never met before. Tamara's parents are in Europe on a fellowship. Tamara's bedroom is in a cupola, facing the ocean. She can hear the waves pounding at night. She discovers some old diaries in the attic that were written by a twelve-year-old girl in the 1880s. The pages are yellowed, crumbly, the ink fine and black. Finally, Tamara meets the ghost of the girl who wrote them. Together they solve a mystery.

This and four other, similar books are what Sarah has ready to check out when her father comes upstairs to meet her at noon.

"You want to eat lunch at the Firehouse?" he asks her.

Sarah nods. The Firehouse is an old stone firehouse that has been redone as a restaurant.

Sarah is wearing her brown turtleneck under her thick knit sweater. She is wearing jeans, boots, a yellow and green striped hat, and a dark green wool coat. Around her neck is a scarf, striped to match her hat, and on her hands are matching mittens. Even with all this clothing, though, she is unprepared for how bitterly cold it is outside the library. The Firehouse is just down and across the square, but she wonders if she can make it there. She wonders how long it takes for a person to freeze to death.

The sun is blindingly bright, glinting off the ice and snow, packed down on the sidewalks around the square. It is far too cold for Sarah and her father to talk as they walk as fast as they can across the square. They are each hunched down into their coats, books clenched under their arms, hands in their pockets, chins tucked in and heads down, breath steaming in the air. It is so cold that tears start in Sarah's eyes, and she can feel her nose turn red and begin to drip. She sniffs up the drip.

Passing the First National Bank Building, Sarah suddenly notices something. In the big marble planter boxes outside the bank, underneath the bare skeletons of the hedges, poking up out of the earth through the white snow, are dozens of bright green points, like crayon tips. Walking as briskly as she can, Sarah turns her head toward them, narrowing her tearing eyes and staring.

Those green tips, she knows, are the beginning of flowers. She is not sure whether they are daffodils or tulips — that is the sort of thing her mother would have known — but she knows that, whatever they are, they will bloom in the spring.

Right now, right here, in the middle of February, here is spring, Sarah marvels.

At the Firehouse, Sarah's father has chili and Sarah has potato soup. They both have grilled cheese sandwiches.

"Can I interest you in dessert?" asks the waiter, after he has cleared away the soup bowls and sandwich plates.

"Well, what do you have?" asks Sarah's father.

"In addition to what's on the menu, we have something very special today," says the waiter proudly. "Believe it or not, the very first fresh strawberries of the season just came in today, and the chef has made fresh strawberry shortcake."

"That's what I'll have," says Sarah's father.

"Me, too, please," says Sarah.

As soon as the waiter goes, Sarah's father says, "Well, I guess they're our spring-in-the-middle-of-winter, those strawberries, eh?"

Sarah nods. She does not tell him that she already found spring, poking out of the snow *under the bushes* in the planters in front of the First National Bank Building.

One night in April, the air is soft and fragrant and warm, and Sarah and her father open every window in the house. A slight breeze blows in, making all the curtains puff out like twirly skirts and riffling the pages of the seed catalogs that lie all over the living room. The whole house is filled with the good smell of brownies baking, made with the recipe that Sarah's mother always used.

"'Honeychile,'" reads Sarah's father from a catalog. "'At last! A miniature watermelon that won't hog the refrigerator! With one of the highest sugar contents ever tested, tiny Honeychile, not much larger than a good-sized cantaloupe, has a crisp, sweet, delicious flesh of bright pink, bursting with juice, and small, non-objectionable seeds. An American All-Star Winner, 1987.'" Her father snorts. "Non-objectionable seeds, indeed," he says.

"Daddy," says Sarah, "I thought we decided on the Sweetie-Pie melon."

"Well," says her father, "this *is* smaller."

"I guess it doesn't really matter," says Sarah, "I mean, watermelons never do that well here anyway."

"How true," says her father sadly. "But this time, I was thinking that if I really load up the watermelon area with sand..."

"Didn't you say that last year?" asks Sarah.

But last year is when Sarah's mother died.

"To tell you the truth," says her father, "I just don't remember whether I did or not."

"Maybe it wasn't last year," says Sarah.

After dinner, Sarah and her father sit on the front porch in the swinging glider and rock back and forth in the gathering dusk. They rock carefully, so as not to slosh Sarah's father's coffee or Sarah's milk. They are each eating a brownie. The first crickets are beginning to whir.

"Spring is easiest," says Sarah.

"Easiest?" says her father.

"Yes," says Sarah. "To find summer in. I mean, you spend a lot of spring planning for summer."

"Oh, like the seed catalogs," says her father.

"Yes," says Sarah. "And where you'll go on vacation, and what you'll do when school's out."

Her father nods. They both sit quietly. The glider creaks just a little.

"It's about a year now," says Sarah's father. A year, he means, since Sarah's mother died.

"I know," says Sarah. "In that way, spring's the hardest. For us personally, I mean. I guess it always will be."

"In two weeks, it'll be a year exactly."

Sarah nods.

"What shall we do?" asks her father. "To mark it?"

"I don't know," says Sarah. "But we should do something."

They swing for a bit.

"I still miss her," says Sarah. "I don't talk about it, but I do. All the time."

"So do I," says her father. "But at least now we *can* talk about it a little."

"Will we always miss her?" asks Sarah.

"Oh, always, I think," says her father. "Always."

"Miss her like this, always?" asks Sarah.

"No," says her father thoughtfully, blotting his mouth with a paper napkin. "No, I think the way we miss her will change as we change. It would have to. I mean, it has already this year, hasn't it?"

Sarah nods. It has, but she can't quite put into words how. She can, at least, sort of think about it now, instead of just coming up against it as she had for so long, unexpectedly, as if you stood up naturally and — *wham* — suddenly hit your head against something absolutely unyielding, like a shelf, say. Sarah thinks back to the book she reshelved at the library. "'It was impossible,'" she says, quoting, "'that anything could ever be the same' after that."

Her father nods, not knowing that she is quoting, taking her small hand in between his two large ones. She puts down her empty glass and leans into him.

"Why did you throw her clothes out, after, Daddy?" she asks him.

"I didn't throw them out, I gave them away. And not all of them. I saved a few, some I thought maybe you'd want to wear someday. But I did get rid of most of them, yes."

"Well, why?"

"The smell of them," he says. "I couldn't..." He stops. "They reminded me too much of..." Sarah feels him tremble with not-quite-crying.

She sniffs her father's smell. Aftershave, the edge of sweat covered with deodorant, and a smell around his face and beard that, as she thinks about it, is a little like the earth they dig in the garden. She can barely remember her mother's smell: a sweet rose perfume, a clean smell of an almond soap, a green herby scent to her hair from the shampoo she used, and, at night, a minty cold cream that smelled a bit like a drugstore or a doctor's office.

"I have to tell you something," she whispers to her father.

He nods.

"The day after the funeral?"

He nods again.

"I went into the bathroom, and there was her hairbrush. And her hair was still in it. And I picked it up and I smelled it. And I took a comb and I started cleaning that hair out of the brush. I went over and over with that comb, to get out all the hair. Then I took tweezers, and I pulled out every single hair — every single one. I got it so it looked like nobody had ever used that brush. Then I washed the brush with shampoo and water."

Sarah is crying now, into her father's warm shoulder as he puts his arm around her, hugging her hard.

Finally she stops crying. She looks up at her father, her face wet. Behind him, she sees the streetlight on the corner has a rainbow-y glow around it from all the tears she has cried. Then she says, "But you know? The hair that I took out of the brush? I couldn't throw it away, just…you know, in the wastebasket. So I took it and sort of made it into a ball, and put the ball in the back of my jewelry box. I haven't taken it out since, but I have it there and I think about it."

Her father says, "I saved that sweater vest, the one with the geese. One of these days you'll be big enough to wear it."

They rock on the glider.

"Daddy," whispers Sarah, "what is the beginning in that ending?"

"In your mother's dying, you mean?" asks her father.

Sarah nods. "Like winter holding spring, and spring holding summer...like that." She leans down to pick up her paper napkin. She blows her nose in it.

Her father sighs a long sigh, and pulls Sarah close to him, so that his arm is around her and she leans against his chest. She can feel his heart beating under his shirt, and one of his buttons presses gently into her cheek.

"Sometimes," he says, "you can't know exactly what the beginning in an ending is, only that there is

one, somehow. Because you see that in everything else, you know there has to be one, even in that."

"But," says Sarah, "you must have some idea, Daddy. What could it be?"

Her father sighs. "Well, with a year, because it's happened before, you can see each beginning very clearly. You know that strawberries come before peaches and peaches before pumpkins and around and around. But with people, with lives..."

He stops.

"With lives?"

"Well, each life is different. Lives don't follow the same patterns, not in the way years do. It's not so

clear. At least, not until later, when you can look back and say, 'Oh, if Ginny hadn't died, I might never have been so close to my daughter Sarah, I never would have known her so well, known how much I loved her.' And there's something about losing someone you love, where it hurts so much that it just burns away a lot that doesn't matter, and you just see things more clearly."

"But that wasn't a *reason* for Mommy to die, Daddy!"

"No, no, Sarah, of course not. But she did, you see — for whatever the reason may be, which we can't know, any more than we can know why the seasons change. But in that end was a new beginning, of our loving each other in a new way... maybe even of a new understanding of what love is. It's hard to say it, and maybe you don't feel this, but an understanding of love itself — beyond the loving some*one*. That's what's left, after the hurt burns so much away."

Sarah thinks about it.

"What else?"

"I don't know if I can put it in words, Sarah. But — it's a beginning to what is ahead, unknown, in the future. People you will meet and love and people I will meet and love ... waiting out there in the future for us, and we will be ready for them, maybe, in some way that we couldn't have been without your mother's love and the sadness of her dying. And maybe one of those people out there in the future someday is your very own daughter."

"Daddy!" Sarah gasps. She is amazed, shocked, intrigued. "I'm only eleven, Daddy."

"But eleven holds twelve, and twelve holds…"

Sarah thinks of springs holding summers, summers falls.

"It goes…" She pauses. "Daddy, when you think about it like that, it goes as far back and as far forward as you can see or think about. Even farther."

Like Tamara and the other heroines in the kinds of books Sarah loves, she feels that she is traveling through time. For a moment, Sarah thinks of grandmothers and great-grandmothers and children and grandchildren and great-grandchildren.

She thinks, My mother is alive in me and always will be.

She thinks, Will she be in my children, too? And will *I* be? Even though I haven't had them yet?

Are they already there, waiting for me? And who else is waiting, and what else? What if I don't have children? Will there be someone to love me, someone I can pass on to — ?

And she feels, suddenly, what her father was saying, about love itself. *I will always be loved,* she thinks solemnly. Then she wrinkles her face. She thinks, No, that's not it exactly. It's more like, *love* is alive in me and always will be.

Sarah feels dizzy as if she had been twirling like she used to when she was a very little girl…like, perhaps, her own little girl would someday…like, perhaps, her mother had done.

Had done?

"Daddy," says Sarah, "do you remember a blue skirt Mommy used to wear, a blue like a swimming pool?"

"Oh, yes," says her father. "I think it was a gauze skirt, very full, sort of aqua-colored. She used to wear it around the house..."

"And she'd put some music on loud, and kind of dance..." says Sarah. "And it would sort of puff out around her..."

"Oh, yes, I remember," says her father. "Your mother was a twirler, all right." He smiles.

"A twirler," repeats Sarah. "And she loved basil. Remember how she loved basil?"

"Oh, yes. Basil on spaghetti. Basil in salad. Basil on tomatoes. Remember how she'd cut it like a bouquet and bury her nose in it and just sniff?"

"Mmmm," says Sarah, agreeing, thinking.

Sarah and her father sit on the glider and rock some more.

"Look!" Sarah suddenly says, pointing. "A firefly! I think that's the first one this year!"

Silently, Sarah and her father watch the firefly. Sarah thinks she has never felt this way before: sad, happy, so much, so at once. *Love is alive in me and always will be,* she thinks, feeling a lifting inside her, and wonders, Has this been here all along, this feeling? Have I just not seen it? Would I ever have seen it without Mommy dying? And for once she hears the question in herself, without feeling disloyal or worrying that it is a terrible question that may not be asked. For her mother is, of course, always part of this love.

"I think," she whispers to her father, "I think we should plant a tomato plant on Mommy's grave. And some basil."

Her father throws back his head. He laughs and laughs and laughs. He hugs Sarah, slaps her on the back, and laughs some more.

"Perfect," he says. "Oh, Sarah, that is perfect."

"But not watermelon," says Sarah a little strictly. "They never do well here."

"No," agrees her father, wiping his eyes. "No, my little honeychile. A plant that doesn't do well would never be right. But I know your mother would love a tomato plant and some basil."

"And in the fall," says Sarah, "some bulbs. Some daffodils and tulips, to come up the next spring, okay?"

"Daffodils, tulips, tomatoes, and basil. Perfect," agrees her father. "I love you, Sarah."

"Did you know," says Sarah, "that those bulbs start to come up sometimes even in the very coldest weather? Right through the snow, even?"

Her father hugs her one more time. "Winter," he whispers into her hair, "holding spring."